5 2004

J FIC Broom

Broome, E.
What a goat!.

PRICE: $4.10 (3587/ux   )

What A Goat!

by Errol Broome
illustrations by Sharon Thompson

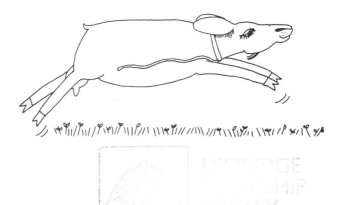

Annick Press Ltd.
Toronto • New York • Vancouver

First published in 1997 by
Fremantle Arts Centre Press, Western Australia

Cataloging in Publication

Broome, Errol
    What a goat! / by Errol Broome ; illustrations by Sharon
Thompson. – North American ed.

(Annick chapter books)
ISBN 1-55037-869-4 (bound).–ISBN 1-55037-868-6 (pbk.)

    1. Goats–Juvenile fiction. I. Thompson, Sharon, 1958- II. Title. III.
Series.

PZ7.B793Wh 2004   j823'.92   C2004-901267-3

The text was typeset in Century Oldstyle.

Distributed in Canada by: Published in the U.S.A. by:
Firefly Books Ltd.   Annick Press (U.S.) Ltd.
66 Leek Crescent   Distributed in the U.S.A. by:
Richmond Hill, ON   Firefly Books (U.S.) Inc.
L4B 1H1   P.O. Box 1338, Ellicott Station
                                   Buffalo, NY 14205

Printed and bound in Canada by Friesens, Altona, Manitoba

visit us at: **www.annickpress.com**

1

That goat will have to go.

Dad said it every time Gerda ate someone's socks or escaped into the neighbors' orchard.

Mostly, Eliza didn't take any notice. Gerda was always getting into scrapes. She caused more trouble than three sheep, five hens, and Harry all put together.

In the small town of Marlock, people kept animals and grew fruit and vegetables. They spun woolen fleeces for sweaters and sold eggs and cream and honey.

Neighbors helped one another. It was Mrs. Mackaffie next door who suggested the Sevilles buy a goat. Eliza was only two years old then and small for her age. "I mean to say, she's a sickly sort of child," said Mrs. Mackaffie. "It's cow's milk that's doing it. Why don't you try a goat?"

So Gerda came into the family. "Gerda was so good while Dad learned to milk her," Mom told Eliza. "It took a week before he got two hands going at the same time. He whistled to her and pretended he was playing the bagpipes—and not once did she kick him or poo in the bucket."

Gerda produced enough milk not just for Eliza but for Mom and Dad too. In less than six months, she had paid for herself in savings on the cost of milk. She had also become part of the family.

Dad made a half-door, like a gate, so Gerda could see over the top into the house. She rested her head on the door and watched Eliza with soft, creamy eyes. *Hm-m-m-m-m*, she said when Eliza stretched up to pat her.

Every morning and every evening Dad milked and whistled until, after two years, Gerda's milk dried up. Eliza was four by then, skipping-strong and big for her age. She didn't need goat's milk anymore.

Sometimes she thought she didn't need a baby brother either. Harry was all right, but a goat was better. Gerda had become Eliza's friend. Wherever Eliza went in the yard, Gerda trotted behind. When Mom was busy with Harry, Eliza sat on an upturned bucket and talked to Gerda. She stroked Gerda's muzzle. It was dewy soft and pink and quivered at her touch. *Hm-m-m-m-m*.

Not everything about Gerda was good, though. Day by day and weeks stretching into months, she chewed through all the trees. Their trunks stood like skeletons in the yard.

Mr. Mackaffie hobbled in from next door

to inspect them. He'd been walking like that since his accident with the cow. "I'm not much use anymore," he muttered. "If I was a horse, they'd have shot me."

He limped from tree to tree, then took off his hat and scratched his head. "Would you believe, ringbarked?"

Mrs. Mackaffie stared at Gerda. "Amazing! I mean to say, how could one goat kill so many trees?"

"That goat will have to go," said Dad.

But instead, he moved Gerda to a yard with the three brown sheep and planted new trees where the old ones had died. He whistled as he admired the row of young poplars, and his toothy grin made Eliza smile too.

Most afternoons, Mom and Eliza took Gerda for a walk. On their way to the nearby oval park, they stopped to talk with other people walking dogs or riding ponies.

The bell on Gerda's collar jingled as she moved. Eliza could tell where Gerda was and what she was doing by the sound of her bell. When it was silent, Gerda was cudding. She lay on the grass, her jaws shifting like a machine from side to side. If the bell tinkled, Gerda was grazing. When it jangled in the air, Gerda was somewhere she shouldn't be, like the morning Eliza found her on the roof of the car. She had

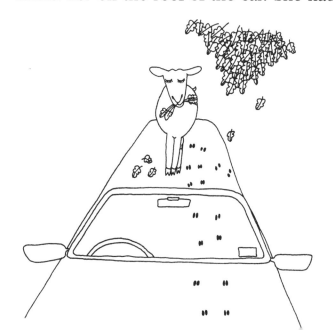

used the hood and roof as a ladder to reach young leaves on the oak tree.

The car looked as if someone had painted an all-over brown and white design. Eliza helped Dad to hose off the muddy hoofprints. "How can I say a goat climbed on the car!" he said as he drove off, late for work. "That goat will have to go."

At school next day, Eliza wrote:

My Dad whistles but not when Gerda walks on his car.

2

Eliza grew and Harry grew and Gerda went on her worrying way. She stretched her neck like a giraffe to nibble leaves around corners. She climbed like a monkey over rocks and gates and fences.

"Next we'll find her up a tree!" said Dad.

Eliza stepped one afternoon into a silent yard. There was no tinkle of the bell, and Gerda wasn't cudding. Empty. Hush. "Gerda's gone!"

Mom's face drained white as milk. "We'd

better find her double-quick, before she does any damage."

It was too late. Someone screamed next door. Mom and Eliza ran down the road, through the gate into the Mackaffies' place. "Wait for me," called Harry as he trailed along behind.

Mr. Mackaffie stood in the orchard behind the house. He pushed his hat back on his head and grunted. "Would you believe, every apple gone!"

Gerda twitched her nose and wagged her tail.

"Gerda likes it here," said Eliza.

"Shhh!" said Mom. "This is trouble!" She mumbled apologies and said she just didn't know what to do with Gerda.

Mrs. Mackaffie strolled across from her sunflower patch. "Gerda beats the grubs this year," she said. "I mean to say . . ." Her words tumbled out like a string of beads. "If it's not one thing, it's another. We get a cow and it kicks old Mac so he's lame for life. The foxes eat all our bantams. We try apples and the grubs get them. Now it's a goat. What next?"

"Oh dear!" Mom sighed as they led Gerda back along the road.

Harry caught up with them and grabbed Eliza's pigtail. "Has Gerda gotta go?"

Eliza caught her breath. "Of course not."

"I don't care," he said. "I only like dogs." Eliza took his hand and they trudged along the dirt road together, Mom and Eliza and Harry and the goat.

"We're lucky to have such good neighbors," said Mom. "How can I ever make up for all the apples they've lost?"

She went straight to the kitchen to make a cheesecake. "It's the least I can do."

When Dad came home, she turned on him like a kettle suddenly come to the boil. "That goat pushed under the fence!" she spurted. "Ate the Mackaffies' apples! I've got better things to do than make cakes! Here I am cooking when we should be building fences!"

Dad didn't say "That goat has to go." He touched Mom gently on the arm as if that might calm her down. "I'll get someone in to build a goat-proof fence. Don't worry. I promise. And till then, we'll tether her."

At school next day, Eliza wrote:

My Mom's a bit grumpy and she says "Oh dear" a lot.

3

They tied Gerda to a post in the middle of the yard. But one day when no one was looking, the rope disappeared. It had not done a rope trick. Gerda had eaten it.

They found her cheerfully chewing sunflowers.

"Gerda!" screamed Eliza.

Gerda trotted across from the neighbors' as if nothing had happened. She rubbed her head against Eliza's leg. "You like it here, don't you?" said Eliza.

"She certainly does," said Mrs.

Mackaffie. "Did I say what next? Well, now we know."

"I'm sorry . . . I'm sorry . . . what else can I say?" said Mom. "Oh dear, Eliza! We can't go on like this."

"We'll have a new fence soon," said Eliza. "A proper fence for goats."

"What you need now, lass, is a good heavy chain," said Mr. Mackaffie. "I've got just the thing in the shed." He limped off, holding his hip and muttering, "If I was a horse, they'd have shot me."

The light faded from the sky as Eliza led Gerda home that afternoon. The yellow day had vanished with the sunflowers.

Dad came in quietly and didn't ask why Mom was baking another cake. He slumped into an armchair.

"The sooner we get that fence, the better," said Mom.

"The fence will have to wait," he said. "I've been laid off."

Mom spun around to face him. "No! Not your job!"

Dad nodded. "From today. Sorry, love. Things are going to be tough around here for a while."

Eliza knew enough about jobs not to say anything. She wanted to ask about the fence. Instead, she said, "Mr. Mackaffie gave us a chain for Gerda."

"Yes," said Mom, trying to be cheerful. "A chain no person or animal can chew through or destroy."

"Good," said Dad in a flat voice.

Gerda didn't find anything good about the chain. The five plump hens pecked and strutted free around her. She soon discovered that if she kept walking around

the post, the chain wound closer and tighter until she could not take another step. She bleated for Eliza to come and let her off.

Gerda nuzzled Eliza's legs. *Hm-m-m-m-m*. Eliza stroked her and then raised a finger. "Don't you do that again!"

Her-er-er-er-er.

Every time Eliza looked out the window, Gerda was wedged beside the post.

"She only does it so you'll go out and talk to her," said Dad.

"But it's horrible being on a chain.

There's no shade—and how can she get away from dogs or snakes?"

"I suppose you're right." Dad agreed to fix the fence himself. He worked on it for days, tightening wires and strengthening posts. In between, he searched the newspapers for jobs and planted seeds of vegetables to grow and sell. All the while he dug and planted and weeded, he tried to work out ways to make extra money. He trudged around town looking for work. He

knocked on doors and asked if he could help mend other people's fences or mow their lawns. His snow peas grew tall and laden with pods, so he sold some to the local greengrocer. But most of the time, his garden barely managed to keep the family in vegetables.

"I don't know what we'll do if something doesn't come up soon," he said.

"We'll manage," said Mom. "I've still got my three days' work at the gallery." But she knew the money from that would not even pay the bills.

Dad grew thin and Eliza saw lines on his face that hadn't been there before.

At school she wrote:

It's not much fun at home when your father's out of work. He doesn't whistle anymore.

4

Gerda was happy to be off the chain. She trotted over to Eliza and tossed her head and bleated. Her tail wagged jauntily.

Dad's patched-up fence kept her inside. For a while.

Then one day, Gerda found the weak spot. She pushed down the wires until she could climb over the top strand.

"Gerda's gone again!" said Eliza.

She knew where to find her. The Mackaffies were under the clothesline when Eliza knocked on the door. "Around the back!" called Mrs. Mackaffie. "Look what's happened now!"

Eliza took a deep breath and walked around the side of the house. Mrs. Mackaffie pointed to an empty line, empty but for a few scraps of cloth dangling from the pegs.

"Would you believe . . ." said Mr. Mackaffie. "Last night we had washing on the line. This morning after breakfast—nothing!"

Someone's had breakfast, thought Eliza, and I know who. "Sorry," she said. "What will you do now?"

Mrs. Mackaffie shook her head. "I mean to say, I don't know what I mean to say."

Mr. Mackaffie shuffled along the line and unpegged the chewed remains of the wash. The pieces fluttered to the ground. He groaned as he bent to pick them up. "If I was a horse, they'd have shot me."

Mrs. Mackaffie gazed at Gerda and sighed. "I don't know whether to laugh or cry. We'll have to do something about Gerda, won't we?"

Eliza nodded and mumbled something that sounded like please or maybe. She hurried Gerda away, but as she neared her own house she slowed to a stop. She didn't want to go home. She knew what Dad would say this time. Things were different now.

Harry leaned out the window and shouted at her.

"Don't bring Gerda back here. She's just a smelly old goat. We don't want Gerda anymore!"

Dad was out fixing the fence again. "Look, Eliza," he said, "that goat has to go."

"No!" she shrieked.

"Shhh," he replied. "We'll talk about it tonight."

Mom, who was standing nearby, put an arm around Eliza's shoulder and spoke to her softly. "We'll do what's best for all of us."

Eliza didn't want to talk about it. She couldn't imagine life without Gerda. She'd been part of their house for eight years. Up until now, every time Dad had said Gerda had to go, she knew he'd forget by morning. Even when Gerda left a pile of droppings like small black marbles at the door. Even when her hay blew up the path and made him sneeze.

But lately a small seed of doubt had stirred in her mind and kept her awake at night. One day, he'd mean it. One day, Gerda would have to go.

She took Gerda to the shed and gave her fresh hay. Gerda nuzzled her head against Eliza's shoulder. Eliza's throat was dry and she couldn't bring herself to speak. She turned instead and laid her cheek against Gerda's face. *Hm-m-m-m-m,* murmured Gerda.

Eliza stood up and wiped her eyes. "It'll be all right," she said.

She walked into the house with her head down. Sometimes, if you didn't look at people, they didn't talk to you. They acted as if you were not there.

But the trick didn't work this time. Mom

caught her by the shoulders and turned her around. "Listen, Eliza. We just can't afford to keep Gerda anymore."

"So . . . you mean Gerda has to go?" Eliza said, chewing on her bottom lip.

Mom nodded. "It's come to this. I'm sorry."

"What about the sheep—and the chickens?"

"We get wool for spinning, and the hens keep us in eggs. Gerda costs money and gives us nothing."

"That's not true!" Gerda was a friend, and friends didn't have to give wool or eggs.

"You know what I mean, Eliza. We haven't got the money to build a strong fence or keep on feeding her—and now we have to buy new sheets for the Mackaffies."

"Why?"

"Because Gerda ate their sheets off the line, that's why. It isn't funny anymore. I'll miss her as much as you will, but we have to face it."

"If we start milking her again, we won't have to buy any milk."

"She's old. Too old to have another kid," said Dad, who was seated at the kitchen table.

"What . . . where will she go then?"

Dad leaned one elbow on the table. "First, we'll try to give her away. But I'm afraid no one's going to want an old nanny goat."

"I'm sorry," said Mom. "None of us wants to see Gerda go."

Harry stuck out his jaw and didn't say a word.

Eliza stared at them and knew her face

was red. "I don't believe you," she shouted. "You never liked her!"

"Now you're being silly," said Mom. "Gerda's been part of the family—still is."

"Then who goes next? Me?"

Dad pushed back his chair and leaped to his feet. "Eliza! Go to bed! You're being absurd."

Eliza knew she was being horrible. She was making things worse for everyone. But she couldn't help it. Gerda had given her milk when she was small. It was her turn now to save Gerda. "All right!" she screamed. "I will go to bed." She stamped out of the kitchen. Tears blurred in her eyes as she groped down the hallway to her room. She threw herself on the bed without taking off her shoes and lay there with her face hidden in the pillow.

She couldn't even fight for Gerda. There

was nothing she could do. She wanted to hide, to block all this from her mind and pretend it was not happening.

The pillow was warm and wet under her cheek. Lying there crying was not helping Gerda. Perhaps there *was* something she could do for her. She could find her a good home.

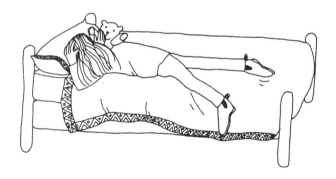

5

"Feeling better?" asked Dad the next morning. Eliza wished they wouldn't ask questions like that. She half-nodded. "If you'll let me find a home for Gerda."

"Why not?" he said. "That's a good idea."

"I'll ask people. And I'll take Gerda with me. She's so nice."

"Dogs are better," said Harry.

"Shut up, Harry. We're not getting a dog."

"I'll give you a week," said Dad. "If we haven't found a place by next Friday, then we'll . . . well, I'll give you a week."

Mom smiled as if a load had been taken from her shoulders. It was a load Eliza had to carry now.

The late spring air pressed heavily around her as she went to the shed to give Gerda fresh water and hay. Gerda bleated and ran to meet her. Snort, nuzzle, butt. Eliza stroked her head. She saw the dull gray hairs among Gerda's whiskers. "But you're not old, are you, Gerda!"

Hm-m-m-m-m.

That day at school she wrote:

I'll do anything if only someone will give my goat a good home.

After school, Eliza put Gerda on a rope and set off to knock on doors.

"Can I come?" asked Harry. His mouth hung open, waiting for her answer.

"If you promise not to talk. You never say anything nice about Gerda."

As they went through the gate, she heard Dad's voice from the house. "Nobody's going to want an old goat."

"Give her a chance to find out," said Mom.

"I'll show them," she said to herself. To Harry she said, "Come on, we haven't got all day."

He skipped beside Eliza as she led Gerda toward the farms in the valley. The road was hard and dusty. Long grass in the ditch crackled like straw when it brushed against their legs. Gerda's head drooped as they walked. She's tired already, thought Eliza.

The first house down the hill hid behind an avenue of oak trees. Eliza led Gerda along the winding driveway. "The Palumbos live here."

A gap in the hedge opened onto the house and garden. Eliza rang the doorbell. She held Gerda and waited.

Mrs. Palumbo opened the door. "Eliza Seville, is it? And . . . er . . . ?"

"Gerda. And this is Harry."

Mrs. Palumbo smiled. "Is something wrong?"

"No—well, yes."

"I'm sorry I can't ask you in, unless you tie up the goat out here."

"Oh, no," said Harry. "She'd eat her rope."

Eliza frowned at him.

"It's a joke," he said feebly.

"I know goats." Mrs. Palumbo looked at Gerda. "And this one looks old."

"Not so old," said Eliza. "That's why we're here. We wondered, would you like a goat? She's a very nice goat, the best goat you'd ever have."

Mrs. Palumbo stepped out of the doorway. "You want to give her away? What a shame! I'd like to make her a home, but we have bees, not animals. We have no fences."

Eliza hung her head. "I see. Thank you, anyway." She turned to go.

"I'm so sorry," Mrs. Palumbo called after her.

Farther along the road, they came to the Montinis' house. Mrs. Montini was always smiling. Eliza knew she'd smile on Gerda too.

She knocked on the door. There was a crash at the other end of the house and a rush of feet up the hall. Paws scuffed against the door. Mrs. Montini called from farther away. "I'm coming!" She opened the door. Two small hairy dogs spilled through the opening.

"We have many animals, as you can see." Mrs. Montini's eyes laughed as she spoke.

"Then would you like a goat—for free?"

Mrs. Montini ran her hand along Gerda's back. "She's a fine goat, but why free?"

"She eats things," said Harry.

Eliza nudged him with her elbow. "Dad's out of work, and we need a new fence."

"Of course. I see. You must find a new home for the goat. I wish it could be here, but if I tell Mr. Montini I've taken in a goat …" She ran her finger across her throat.

"She'll eat all your weeds," said Eliza, but she could tell the Montinis didn't need a goat.

"Perhaps the Dunstans over the hill would take her," said Mrs. Montini as they walked away.

Eliza's legs were aching and her shoes pinched her toes. Gerda dragged her feet and almost tripped on the gravel path. She is getting old, thought Eliza. Then she pushed the thought away.

"When can we go home?" asked Harry.

"Not yet." Her voice was dull and heavy. "You shouldn't have come if you can't last the whole way." She was beginning to wonder if anyone wanted Gerda.

"What if no one takes her?" asked Harry, as if he knew what Eliza was thinking.

"I'm not sure." She hadn't thought that far ahead. Or if she had, she'd pushed it to the back of her mind. "We'll try one more place today, before we go home."

They crossed the road and followed a short track to the horse farm. The Duracks could afford to keep Gerda, thought Eliza. The well-kept wooden fences were painted white and a sign across the entrance said DURACK STUD FARM.

A bell rang when Eliza opened the gate. She and Harry and Gerda trudged up the drive between neat fences with horses grazing on both sides. Before they reached the main building, a man came out of a shed. "Hello there. You lost or something?"

"No, we're looking . . ."

"So you've lost *something*."

"We're looking for a home for Gerda."

The man put a hand under his chin and spread his fingers across his mouth. "Ahem, hmmm." His brow furrowed as he stared at the three figures in front of him. "Then who's Gerda?"

"She's our goat."

The man let out a long breath. "I could've guessed. What's she done wrong?"

Eliza sidestepped to block Harry before

he could speak. "We can't look after her anymore," she said.

"That's tough, kid. Look, I could ask the boss, but I can tell you now, he won't have a goat around here. If it was a pony, that'd be a different matter. But a goat! We've got no goat fences here. She'd be off before you could say Seabiscuit."

He looked from Gerda to the children. "Sorry, kids. You got a long way to go home?"

His understanding voice made Eliza realize how tired she was. Drained by disappointment. Nobody wanted an old goat, and Gerda did look old today. "We'll be all right," she replied, though she didn't feel all right at all.

Nobody at school wanted Gerda either, or if they did, their parents wouldn't allow it. After school each day, Eliza walked the road out of Marlock with Gerda beside her. Everyone had the same reply. They'd like to help out . . . but, sorry.

If only they could see how beautiful she was, with her creamy coat and soft, friendly eyes. No one would notice the gray hairs around the chin. "Look at her pretty face. . ." she'd say. "Listen how she talks to you. . . . She's my best friend, after Mom and Dad and Harry."

Eliza begged people to take Gerda, and yet she didn't want her to go. She felt like a rag doll, pulled one way and then another. Torn apart.

6

On her way home from school on Friday, Eliza met Mr. Mackaffie outside the store. He hobbled beside her to the start of the road home. "Go along, don't wait for me," he said. "If I was a horse, they'd have shot me."

Eliza was not in a hurry to get home. She'd failed to find a home for Gerda and she dreaded what Mom and Dad would do next.

"Mr. Mac . . ." The breath caught in her

throat and she couldn't say any more.

"Yes, lass." He stopped on the side of the road and looked down at her.

"I . . . er . . . oh, it's nothing. I can't . . . I can't . . . Mr. Mackaffie, nobody wants Gerda."

Mr. Mackaffie placed his hand on her shoulder. "Let's walk together, then. I'm due home, you know, to help babysit the grandson. By now, Mrs. Mac will be fed up good and proper with the little tyke. He never sits still; wants to spend all day in the park—runs off all the time."

"Like Gerda." Eliza smiled at the thought. "Getting through fences too?"

"Of course. It's easy for a three-year-old. He wants to see what's on the other side."

"Like Gerda." It always came back to Gerda. Eliza couldn't get her out of her mind. "Everything's gone wrong."

"You think it's the end of the world right now," said Mr. Mackaffie, "but it's the way things go. Something comes along next day and life goes on."

"Like Dad's work. Do you think he'll get another job?"

" 'Course he will. It's the not knowing that's getting him down. One day, it will all come right again."

"Then why do we have to give up Gerda?"

Mr. Mackaffie coughed, a thinking-what-to-say sort of cough. "Because right now, Eliza, things are in a bad way, and we've just got to do what's best."

Eliza dawdled along the road, watching her feet as she put one brown shoe in front of the other.

Mr. Mackaffie's voice was gentle. "Gerda's had a good run, you know. More than eight years you've had her, and given her a fine home. Nothing lasts forever. Everything changes—sometimes it's slow, like growing old, or it may only take a minute, like this leg of mine."

Eliza tugged at his arm, so that he stopped. She didn't look at him as she spoke. "Mr. Mackaffie, if . . . if you were a goat, would they shoot you?"

He smiled. Then, as quickly as it had come, the smile vanished from his face. "Now, Eliza, what makes you ask a thing like that?"

She turned her face to him and it was streaked with tears. "I think . . . I know . . . I heard them talking."

"I wouldn't like to say," he said. "No, I think that's a question for your parents."

Eliza bit her lip and stared ahead as they neared the rambling hedge outside the

Mackaffies' place. She saw the gap in the greenery and then a small figure running along the shoulder toward them.

"By jiminy!" said Mr. Mackaffie. "It's the little tyke!" He tried to move faster, dragging his stiff leg after the other.

"It's who?"

"Fergie. He's out again. Grab him, will you, Eliza, before he runs on the road."

Eliza ran ahead and scooped the small boy into her arms. He kicked and giggled. She handed him to Mr. Mackaffie.

"I bet your nana's looking for you," he said. "We'll have to lock you up, young fellow." He stood

Fergie on the ground and held his hand as they walked toward the Mackaffies' house.

"Park!" said Fergie. "Grandpa, come to the park?"

"Maybe in the morning," said Mr. Mackaffie. "A swing and a slide in the morning, eh?" He stopped at his gate. "Well, here we are now, and a good thing too."

Eliza walked on home with her head to one side, listening. The house was quiet. Only Gerda said hello. She plodded across the yard and wagged her ears at Eliza. *Her-er-er-er-er*.

Eliza stroked her head. "Where is everyone?"

The back door was locked and nobody answered when she called. She turned a bucket upside down and sat on it. Gerda put her head on Eliza's shoulder.

"You're my best friend," she said. Once, Gerda had been fun. Now she was as comfortable as an old cushion. It made Eliza feel good to come home to her. "I won't let anything happen to you."

Hm-m-m-m-m.

Footsteps scrunched on the path and Mom hurried to the door with a load of shopping. "Sorry. I was held up at the gallery."

"Where is everyone?"

"Harry's off playing at the Stubbs' and Dad's out looking for work."

"Good."

Mom unlocked the door and pushed it open with her bags. "What do you mean, good?"

"It'll be good if he finds it." She was thinking of Gerda.

Mom nodded. "Poor Dad. It's harder on him than anyone."

That's what you think, thought Eliza.

7

Eliza sat at the kitchen table and spread honey on her toast while Gerda watched over the half-door. "I walked home with Mr. Mackaffie. They've got their grandson there."

"Fergie's staying the weekend. We should offer to look after him for a while."

"No, thanks," said Eliza. She had enough worries of her own.

Dad came home with a crumpled face.

"No luck?" said Mom.

"I'm wearing out my shoes, that's all I'm doing."

Eliza waited for him to say something about Gerda. For a few moments, there was silence. Her heart sounded as if it were beating in her ear.

Then Dad sighed. "We'll have to talk about Gerda. When Harry gets home, we'll decide."

"Why Harry? He never wanted a goat."

"We need a family discussion, and Harry is part of the family. I want to make sure we all understand."

Eliza hoped Harry would be late getting home. The Stubbs might ask him to stay the night. Or perhaps he'd get one of his stomachaches and be too sick to talk. Dad would have to put off the discussion.

But Harry marched in at six o'clock with a grubby face and a grin. Mom pointed to the bathroom. "After you wash, we'll have dinner and then . . ."

"Then we can talk," said Dad.

After dinner, they sat in the small family area off the kitchen. Eliza wanted to run away, but there was no way out now. It was like sitting for her worst exam.

She heard Gerda rapping on the half-door. If she craned her neck, she could see Gerda's face watching them. Listening?

Dad's hands gripped the arms of his chair. "I'm not enjoying this," he began, "but I don't want you to think Gerda just disappeared. You'd spend the rest of your lives wondering where she went and what happened to her." He drummed his fingers on the chair. "Mom and I have talked about this, and we haven't found a good answer. The thing is . . . we're running out of money. The job at the gallery hardly pays for our food each week. We can't keep Gerda because we can't afford a decent fence. And we can't go on buying hay and goat pellets and paying for the damage she does when she gets out."

"I've got $23 in my piggy bank," said Eliza.

"It wouldn't last us for a week," said Dad. "We've thought of everything. We tried to find a home for Gerda, but the truth is, nobody wants an old nanny goat."

"So what now?" Eliza wished Dad would stop talking.

Mom watched Dad's face and did not look at Eliza.

"You must know, Eliza . . ." he went on.

"People do it with dogs. We have to face it. We must put her down."

Harry swung his legs and kicked the chair. "What's 'put her down'?"

Eliza knew.

Mom reached out to hold Harry's legs still.

"It's . . . well, we put animals to sleep," said Dad.

"You mean they die?"

Dad nodded.

"Why?"

Dad coughed. "It's kinder that way—better than letting them starve or sending them to a cruel home."

"How do they go to sleep?"

"Well," said Dad slowly, "I think I should do it."

Eliza knew Mr. Mackaffie had a gun. He sometimes used it to scare birds away from his orchard.

"Do we all agree, then?" said Dad.

Eliza knew that nothing she could say would make any difference.

"All right, then," he said. "I'll go and see Mr. Mackaffie in the morning."

Gerda tapped gently on the door.

"Let her in," said Mom.

For the last time.

Eliza opened the half-door and Gerda straggled into the room. She walked to Dad with her head down and stood in front of his chair, not looking at him. He reached out his hand and stroked her neck. Gerda stepped forward and laid her head against his knee.

The family watched and nobody spoke. Gerda moved across and pressed her muzzle against Mom's leg. "Good night," whispered Mom and looked away.

Harry kicked the chair and knew it was

his turn to say good-bye. He put out his hand to pat her head. Gerda rested her head on his knees.

"I like you, really," he said.

Then she came to Eliza. Eliza wrapped her arms around Gerda's neck. Gerda licked her face with her big, pink tongue. *Hm-m-m-m-m*.

People called Gerda a silly old goat and a smelly old goat and sometimes a hairy old goat. She was all these things, but Eliza loved her more than ever today.

"Take her out now," said Mom.

Eliza stood up. Her eyes were dry. And she hadn't said good-bye. She had already decided what to do.

8

Before she went to bed, Eliza chose an apple from the fruit bowl, but she did not eat it. She took her coat from the closet and hung it on her bedroom door. The apple went into one of the pockets, along with a flashlight. Then she emptied her piggy bank and poured the coins into another pocket.

The clammy night closed around her, but she could not sleep. She lay under a sheet and listened. Would Mom and Dad never go to bed? She heard them talking in the kitchen, on and on and on, and then Mom played her favorite music, and it was as if they too wanted to put off the morning.

At last she heard them in the bathroom and bedroom and then there was silence. In the dark, Eliza tiptoed from her bed and pulled on her jeans and a sweatshirt. She picked up her sneakers and coat and crept along the hallway in her socks. The back door clicked when she opened it. Eliza stopped, holding her breath, but nothing moved in the house. She put on her sneakers and stepped into the night.

The yard was streaked with moonlight and shadows.

Gerda slept in a corner of the shed. She stood up when she heard Eliza at the door. *Hoff-off-off-off-off*, she snorted.

"Shhh," whispered Eliza. "We're going away. First thing is to take off that bell." She filled a sack with fresh hay and pulled on her coat. Then she tied a rope to Gerda's collar and led her out of the shed and across the field to the gate.

An owl called as they stepped onto the road. *Hooot! Hooot!* It was comforting to know they were not completely alone. "I'm not scared when I'm with you," said Eliza.

They walked side by side along the road out of town. Gerda's hoofs clip-clopped softly on the dirt at the edge of the pavement. Nothing stirred in the houses. Except for an owl, the world was asleep. Eliza was glad it was night and there was nobody to ask questions.

The distance seemed greater in the dark. She didn't know how long they'd been walking when they reached the oval. They'd be safe there for the night.

Some people called the oval a park, because it had a swing and a slide in one corner and a creek running along the bottom. On hot days, children paddled in the clear, cool water.

Eliza led Gerda to a small hut, where parents and children sometimes sheltered from the rain. It had no door or windows, just an open entrance and bench seats on three sides. She carefully tied Gerda's rope to a bench seat. Then she eased the sack from her shoulder and spread her coat on the ground. She sat down. "Sorry, Gerda, you'll have to sleep on the dirt. The hay's for breakfast."

Hm-m-m-m-m.

She switched on the flashlight and looked at her watch. Twenty past one. Already she was hungry, but the apple had to wait until morning. She wished she'd brought more food. The money was there in her pocket, but she couldn't go into a store before she was well away from Marlock.

Gerda dropped to her knees and lay on the earth floor. Eliza leaned her head against Gerda's neck. "You're okay, aren't you, Gerda? You've had fun. I'm glad you did all those things, like eating the apples and the sunflowers and the sheets."

Hm-m-m-m-m.

"Go to sleep now. We've got a long day

tomorrow." Eliza took off her shoes and socks and curled up on her coat, using the sack of hay as a pillow. She lay and looked at the stars. If only they could tell her where to go tomorrow. First thing in the morning, they must move on. Where, she wasn't sure, but they couldn't go back home. If they just kept on going, then, as Mr. Mackaffie said, something might turn up.

She heard Gerda's soft snort and blow and smelled the warmth of her closeness. Gerda trusted her. It felt good to be here, just the two of them. She should try to sleep, she knew, but her mind was too full of things that she couldn't sort into the right order. They flashed on and off like pictures, all over the place: a road going nowhere, Gerda's eyes watching over the door, Gerda on the roof of the car, Mom's drawn face, Gerda munching in the orchard, Harry's mouth screwed into a question mark, Dad with a gun . . .

9

A car swished past on the road and was gone. Eliza looked at her watch. It was seven minutes past six. She was sure her eyes had not closed, but she must have slept, because sometime in the night Gerda had eaten her socks.

Gerda sat beside her, watching with her friendly eyes. Her jaw chomp-chomped from side to side. Oh well, they weren't very nice socks! Eliza scooped some hay from the sack. "This is better."

The apple might have to last all day, so Eliza took a bite and chewed slowly. She put half back in her coat pocket. They'd have to get moving soon. The family might have missed them by now.

Eliza put her shoes on, stood up, and untied Gerda's rope from the bench. Gerda butted her in the chest.

"Stop it!"

Gerda didn't stop.

"What's wrong then?" Eliza stood up to look and listen.

A triangle of light slanted through the shed opening. Outside, tree trunks glowed in the sunrise. Starlings shrieked from the poplar trees.

For a moment, Eliza thought she heard another voice out there, a small cry lost among the sounds of morning.

But no, it was water gurgling in the

creek, or sparrows chattering from the bushes.

As she stood, Gerda pushed past her legs and nearly knocked her over.

"Hey!" cried Eliza.

Gerda sped between the trees and across the oval toward the creek.

"Stop! Wait! Not that way!" Eliza wanted to travel in the shelter of trees, where they could hide from cars or the day's first joggers. But already Gerda had left her behind. She rushed across the center of

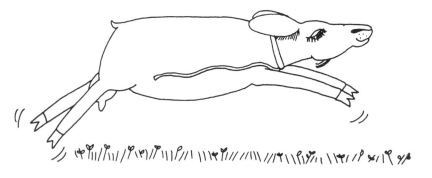

the oval in full view of the road, taking no notice of Eliza's call. She moved as she hadn't moved for months, without a limp or a stumble.

Eliza ran after her, and as she ran she heard the voice again. Singing or crying.

Gerda stopped at the creek and stamped her foot. She turned back to Eliza and bleated. It was a cry to Eliza to come. Come. Quickly. Eliza knew before she reached the creek that there was something in the water.

A small figure in pajamas wallowed in the shallows.

"Hey!" yelled Eliza. "It's the little tyke!"

Fergie floundered and thrashed with his arms as he struggled to stand. "Wah!" He gulped and sank under the water. Again he splashed and kicked and gurgled.

Eliza leaped into the creek and paddled

toward him. The water was above her knees. Her jeans clung to her shins. She reached down and grabbed Fergie with both hands. He struggled and fought and gasped as she dragged him to the bank and set him on his feet. He began to bawl.

"It's all right," she said. "You're all right now."

"Wah!"

"Shhh. You're safe."

"Wah!"

"Shut up!" she snapped. "And what do you think you're doing here? In one more minute, you'd have drowned."

"Wah!" His nose streamed and his face screwed into a giant wail.

"You're sopping wet too." She stared at him. "Now what are we going to do?"

Gerda had forgotten the danger and was drinking from the creek. Eliza shook her head at her. "We're in a real mess, Gerda. What can we do with him?"

Fergie had ruined all her plans. She couldn't leave him here by himself. Within minutes, he'd fall in the creek again or run onto the road in front of a car. She and Gerda were stuck with him. They had to get him home safely.

She glared at the small child and tried not to hate him. She bit her bottom lip. "Because of you . . . because of you, Fergie, Gerda will have to go . . ." The words snagged on her gritted teeth.

She grabbed Gerda's rope and took Fergie by the hand. He squirmed and pulled away.

"You're coming!" she said. "Whether you like it or not!"

10

They began to walk out of the park.

Eliza looked up and saw Mrs. Mackaffie racing down the slope across the oval toward them. Mr. Mackaffie stumbled along behind.

"Thank goodness we've found him." Mrs. Mackaffie began to cry. "He was gone when I went to his room this morning. Oh, when I think what could have happened!" She closed her eyes as if she couldn't bear to see what jumped into her mind.

Fergie yelled and blew dribble at his grandmother.

Mr. Mackaffie huffed and puffed across the grass. "He's all wet . . . he might have drowned."

Mrs. Mackaffie took out her handkerchief and wiped her nose. "Don't tell me, Mac, I know."

"Eliza," said Mr. Mackaffie, "it wasn't you . . . ? Did you save Fergie from the creek?"

Eliza squinted up at them. "It was Gerda, really."

"You're not saying Gerda rescued him?" Mr. Mackaffie scooped Fergie into his arms. "Gerda—truly?"

"She told me," said Eliza. "She showed me where to look."

Mr. Mackaffie wrapped Fergie warmly

against his chest. "What would we have done without Gerda, eh? You're a lucky boy, you little tyke."

"And Eliza," added Mrs. Mackaffie. She put an arm around Eliza's shoulder. "Thank goodness for Eliza."

Mr. Mackaffie turned back to Eliza.

"Now, lass, would you mind telling me how you came to be here?"

"I . . . er . . . we . . ."

Voices called from the road, and Mom and Dad came running through the trees.

Their faces were twisted in a mixture of anger, worry, and relief.

"Oh, Eliza, how could you!" Tears ran down Mom's cheeks.

Why is everyone crying? thought Eliza. I should be the one who's crying.

Harry caught up with them. "What are we all here for?"

Mrs. Mackaffie began to laugh.

"You frightened the life out of us," said Dad. "Disappearing like that."

"It was lucky for us that she did," said Mr. Mackaffie. "She saved Fergie, you know . . . from the creek."

Eliza looked up at her mother. "It wasn't just me. I only pulled him out."

"It was Gerda," said Mrs. Mackaffie.

"Gerda!"

"Yes, Gerda," said Mr. Mackaffie. "You never know with goats." He leaned toward his wife. "Which brings me to something else. Mrs. Mac and I have been thinking. What with the little tyke escaping all the time, we talked about building a stronger fence. She's always had a soft spot for goats, would you believe, and I'd say this has just about made her mind up. We're thinking about going in for angoras."

He pushed back his hat and wiped his hand across his head. "Yes, goats. Now, it wouldn't be any trouble to have Gerda in with them. After what she did this morning, it's the least we can do."

"You mean . . . you mean you'd have Gerda?" said Eliza.

"That's what we're saying, lass."

"So she could stay?"

"Stay she will. We'll have a truly goat- and Fergie-proof fence."

They walked together across the grass

to the gate. When they reached the road, Dad began to whistle. He pointed to Eliza's shoes and winked. "You mean to say you went off without any socks!"

"Who's coming in the car?" asked Mom. "Gerda and I will walk," said Eliza. "It isn't that far." It never seemed far when you were going home.

At school Eliza wrote:

Gerda's going to live next door but she'll always be our goat.

About the author

Errol Broome grew up in Perth, Australia, where she studied Arts at the University of Western Australia and worked as a journalist at the *West Australian*. She is now an award-winning author of more than a dozen books, including *Magnus Maybe* and *Drusilla the Lucky Duck*. Errol lives in Melbourne, Australia.